For Annie, my favorite witch.

Tundra Books, an imprint of Penguin Random House Canada Young Readers,
a division of Penguin Random House of Canada Limited

Published by Tundra Books, 2021
First published by Koyama Press, 2018

Library and Archives Canada Cataloguing in Publication

Title: Evie and the truth about witches / John Martz.
Names: Martz, John, 1978- author.
Identifiers: Canadiana (print) 20200327054 | Canadiana (ebook) 20200327062
ISBN 9780735271005 (hardcover) | ISBN 9780735271012 (EPUB)
Classification: LCC PN6733.M37 E95 2021 | DDC j741.5/971—dc23

Published simultaneously in the United States of America by Tundra Books of
Northern New York, an imprint of Penguin Random House Canada Young Readers,
a division of Penguin Random House of Canada Limited

Library of Congress Control Number: 2020945216

Designed by John Martz
The artwork in this book was created digitally.
The text was set in Plantin.

Printed and bound in China

www.penguinrandomhouse.ca

1   2   3   4   5   25   24   23   22   21

Penguin
Random House
tundra   TUNDRA BOOKS

EVIE
AND THE
TRUTH ABOUT
WITCHES

by John Martz

tundra

Evie wanted to be scared.

"I want to be scared," said Evie
  to the shopkeeper.

"I think you will find what you
  are looking for," said the shopkeeper.

Evie looked, and she looked,
  until finally she saw it.

"THE TRUTH ABOUT WITCHES,"
said the shopkeeper.
"An interesting choice."

The shopkeeper handed
the book to Evie.

"Consider it a gift,"
said the shopkeeper.
"From one reader to another.
But you must promise me
to never . . .
ever . . .
read the last page out loud."

That night, after the rest of her family
had fallen asleep, Evie stayed awake
to read THE TRUTH ABOUT WITCHES.

All night long Evie read stories
about witchcraft and witches,
and all their terrible deeds:
casting dangerous spells,
brewing deadly potions,
and eating kidnapped children
for their supper.

Evie was almost asleep when
she reached the last page
of the book.

There were three strange words,
printed in deep, red ink,
underneath the title
"THE SUMMONING SPELL."

Evie remembered what
the shopkeeper had said,
but she ignored the warning
and began to read the words
out loud.

Prex!

Voco!

Malus!

Nothing happened.

Evie wanted to be scared,
but this book did not scare her.

It did, however, make
Evie feel very, very tired.

She yawned, dropped the book,
and fell into a deep, deep sleep.

Evie was unable to speak.

She did not know why

an old woman was standing

at the foot of her bed.

As if under a spell,
Evie took the woman's hand,
and together they climbed
out the window.

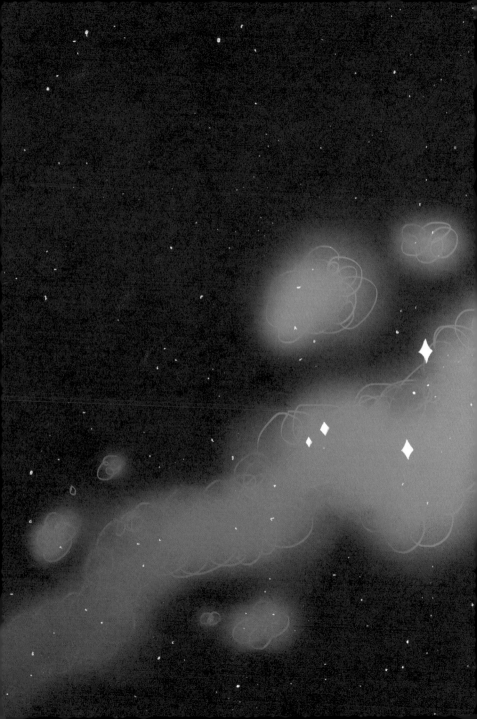

Evie found herself in a strange land.

There were strange plants,

and even stranger animals,

everywhere she looked.

The old woman let go
of Evie's hand and said,
"It is no use trying to run away."

Evie tried to move her feet,
but she could not. She was stuck.

"Why can't I move?" asked Evie.

The old woman wiggled her fingers.
"Magic," she said. "Now, follow me."

Evie felt her feet begin to move again,
and she followed the old woman
deep into the forest.

"Magic?" said Evie.
"I knew you were a witch!"

"No time for chitchat,"
said the old woman.
"We are very, very late,
and the other witches must be
getting very, very hungry.
We must hurry!"

Evie remembered the stories in

THE TRUTH ABOUT WITCHES.

"Please do not eat me!" she said.

"Eat you?" said the old woman.

"Nobody is going to eat you."

"But you said the other witches
   must be getting hungry," said Evie.

"Disgusting!" said the old woman.
"Witches do not eat children!
   Let me show you."

"What is all this?" asked Evie.

"This is all for you," said the
old woman.

"I just finished reading a book
  about everything there is
  to know about witches," said Evie.
"And it did not mention anything
  about parties or cakes."

"Do you believe everything you read?"
  asked the old woman.
"We know all about that awful book.
  Do we seem very scary to you?"

"No," said Evie. "You do not
  seem very scary at all."

"I promise you that we do not
eat children," said the old woman.

"And I promise that our potions
are never poisonous," she said.

"And you really can do magic?"
said Evie.

"We can do so many things,"
said the old woman.

"Being a witch seems like such fun.
Can I be a witch too?" asked Evie.

The old woman smiled and said,
"What a terrific idea!
I wish I had thought of it."

"What must I do?" asked Evie.

"Stand perfectly still,"
said the old woman.

The other witches gathered around.

44

"Am I a witch now?" asked Evie.
She did not feel any different.

"Hmmm," said the old woman.
"Something's not quite right."

She took off her hat
and placed it on Evie's head.

"There!" said the old woman.
"Now you are a witch!"

"I look just like you now," said Evie.

The old woman smiled and said,
"Isn't that funny?"

"What will my parents think
when I tell them I am a witch?"
said Evie.

"Your parents?" said the old woman.
"What do you mean?"

"I have to tell my parents I am a witch when I get home," said Evie.

The witches all stopped smiling,
and for the first time, Evie was scared.

"Home?" said the old woman.

"I'm afraid that is impossible."

"Once you become a witch,
you can never go home again."

"We warned you not to
read the last page."

THE SUMMONING SPELL

Prex

Voco

Malus